ANTHONY MASTERS

The Curse of
the Ghost Horse

Illustrated by Alan Marks

MACDONALD YOUNG BOOKS

Text copyright © Anthony Masters 1999
Illustrations copyright © Alan Marks 1999

First published in Great Britain in 1999
by Macdonald Young Books
an imprint of Wayland Publishers Ltd
61 Western Road
Hove
East Sussex
BN3 1JD

Find Macdonald Young Books on the internet at
http://www.myb.co.uk

The right of Anthony Masters to be identified as the author
and Alan Marks the illustrator of this Work has been
asserted by them in accordance with the
Copyright, Designs and Patents Act 1988

Designed and Typeset by Don Martin
Printed in Hong Kong by Wing King Tong Co. Ltd.

British Library Cataloguing in Publication Data available

ISBN: 0 7500 2653 7 (pb)

CHAPTER ONE

The horses whinnied in their stables and
stamped their hooves. The rabbits stood on
their hind legs shivering, pressing quivering
noses to the wire of their cages. A dog
whined in the yard of Blackhill Stables.

In the house, the frightened cats had already found hiding-places, and out in the fields the sheep huddled together under a great oak for safety.

Far away was the menacing sound of thundering hooves. Alice and Ben looked round uneasily, but strangely there was no sign of a galloping horse.

"Black Bess must be riding out," muttered their cousin Jake Jenkins.

"Who's Black Bess?" asked Ben.

"Our ghost horse." Jake grinned coldly as he walked away. The grin didn't reassure the others.

"Ghost horse?" laughed Ben. "There's no such thing."

"Are you winding us up?" demanded Alice.

The sound of hooves seemed to grow louder and louder, almost beating in time to Ben and Alice's thundering hearts. Suddenly it stopped.

There was a long silence. Then the dog began to bark.

Ben and Alice cantered their Welsh ponies,
Thunder and Lightning, along the ridge.

Down in the valley they could see Blackhill
Stables rising out of the mist.

They had come to stay with Jake while his father was in hospital. He was desperately ill after a riding accident and had slipped into a coma. Aunt Megan sat with him every day.

But Jake didn't want their company. He wanted to ride alone. They could see him now, galloping his horse Diamond along the bottom of the valley towards the Raglan Gap.

"What *is* this stupid legend about the curse of Black Bess?" demanded Ben, reining in Thunder.

Alice came alongside him on Lightning. "Jake wouldn't say anything, as usual."

"Let's ask Alan. He'll know."

"That legend's a load of rubbish," said Alan Jones, the manager of Blackhill Stables.

"But you're going to tell us, aren't you?" pleaded Ben as they led Thunder and Lightning to their loose boxes.

Alan frowned, and then, as he started to speak, Ben and Alice saw the horses were getting restless again. The chickens in the yard were clucking loudly and a dark cloud was passing slowly over the sun.

"Bess was a beautiful black mare that belonged to one of Jake's ancestors – Squire Jenkins. One night down at the inn, he took a bet that Bess could jump the Raglan Gap. But she didn't quite manage it, and they both plunged to their deaths."

"Isn't that where Jake rides every day?" whispered Ben.

But Alice, who was watching one of the horses rattling its loose box door, didn't want to stop Alan in mid-flow. "What happened then?" she asked.

"Squire Jenkins's family cut off Bess's black silky mane as a keepsake, but no one knows where they hid it. The legend goes that Black Bess's ghost roams the Raglan Gap searching for her mane. Until she finds it, the Jenkins family is cursed."

Alan Jones paused. "I don't believe a word of it, but if you look back over the years, there have been an awful lot of accidents."

"What's that noise?" Ben gulped. He thought he'd heard a distant whinny.

"Your imagination," snapped Alan.

The whinny came again, and this time Alice heard it too. The sound seemed to echo in her head.

CHAPTER TWO

That night Alice dreamt about Squire
Jenkins galloping down the track towards
Raglan Gap. Steam came from Black Bess's
flanks and nostrils, dust flew from her
hooves and her eyes were wide with fear.

At breakfast Jake was gloomy and silent as
usual, but then he asked, "How about you
two coming riding with me this morning?"

"Terrific," said Ben.

"Great idea." Alice was thrilled that their cousin was being friendly at last. "Where are we going?"

Jake gave them a faint grin. "To Raglan Gap, of course."

As they cantered Diamond, Thunder and Lightning down the dusty track, Jake was silent. Then he suddenly shouted over his shoulder, "I'm going to find Bess."

"But she doesn't exist," yelled Alice.

"I'm sure I saw her on the other side of the gap. I have to find her mane so she'll lift the curse and let Dad live."

"Alan says that legend's rubbish," shouted Ben. "Surely you can't be so stupid as to believe in a ghost horse!"

The track was getting narrower, heading towards a sharp corner and Jake reined in, the dust rising as he brought Diamond to a sudden halt.

Jake gazed at them wildly and Alice and
Ben stared back. How could he fool himself
like this?

But before they could say anything more,
Jake lightly touched Diamond with his heels
and the horse reluctantly began to walk on.
Ben and Alice could see that his ears were
laid back in fear. So were Thunder and
Lightning's.

"We'll have to ride single-file," warned
Jake. "This place is dangerous."

Ben shivered and Alice gasped in disbelief. They were looking down at a deep gorge through which a fast river flowed, jagged rocks rearing out of the lashing water.

How could anyone – horse or rider – jump that, wondered Alice. The gap between the two smooth rocks was at least three metres and no one could possibly survive the plunge down into the torrent.

Ben imagined Black Bess and Squire Jenkins hurtling down towards the rocks.

They dismounted, watching the churning river below. The other side of the Raglan Gap was shrouded in dense mist.

Then, above the noise of the water, Ben heard the thundering of hooves.

Jake stared desperately into the mist which seemed to be thickening. "I'm going to find her," he shouted. "Bess is always on the other side of the gap."

"Don't be a fool," snapped Ben. "She doesn't exist."

Jake spun round in his saddle. "You don't know anything," he sneered.

"Let's go round," yelled Alice, trying to calm him down.

"It'll take too long. Besides, Bess will expect me to jump."

"Why?" demanded Ben.

But Jake didn't reply, and to their horror he mounted Diamond.

"You'll both be killed!" bellowed Alice.

But Jake wasn't listening, breaking into a trot as Alice made a hopeless grab for the reins.

CHAPTER THREE

As Jake turned Diamond to start the gallop towards the Raglan Gap, they heard the harsh cry of a pheasant and saw rabbits scampering fearfully through the undergrowth.

Jake urged Diamond on, nearer and nearer to the edge, until they were almost lost in the mist. Then Ben and Alice heard a shrill whinny and they could just see Diamond rearing up.

Jake turned back, patting Diamond's neck, trying to reassure him as he prepared for another attempt.

"We've got to stop this," said Alice, and they both tried to block Jake's way with their horses.

But Jake simply swerved Diamond past them, riding towards the spray much faster than before.

Diamond whinnied in terror but still kept galloping as Jake dug in his heels.

Almost immediately, like an echo, an answering whinny followed. Alice glanced at Ben fearfully.

"Look!" Ben's voice was trembling. "Just look at that!"

On the other side of the Raglan Gap, swathed in mist, was the eerie shadow of a beautiful black mare. But there was something odd about her, thought Alice. Then she realized that the horse had no mane.

For a moment, Ben and Alice thought that
Jake and Diamond were going to clear the
gap, but at the very last moment the horse
came to a skidding halt, just on the edge of
the drop. Jake almost fell, just saving himself
by clinging to Diamond's mane.

The whinny from the other side of the
Raglan Gap seemed to go on echoing inside
their heads for a very long time. We were
wrong, thought Ben, his heart thumping
painfully. There *is* a ghost horse out there.

They all three rode home silently over the
ridge and down into the darkening valley.
Jake was furious and brooding, while Ben
and Alice cast sideways glances at him.

Both Ben and Alice admired Jake for his
bravery, but they were terrified that he would
go on trying to jump the Raglan Gap until
he and Diamond eventually plunged to their
deaths – just as Squire Jenkins and Bess had
done.

"It's no good jumping the gap until we've found her mane," pleaded Ben.

"We'll help you," insisted Alice. "We'll all start searching tomorrow."

"By the time we find it, Dad will be dead," said Jake scornfully. "Now shut up, both of you."

As they galloped back through the shadows an owl hooted mournfully and there was the sharp bark of a fox.

When they passed the pond just before the gate of Blackhill Stables, Alice and Ben could hear an urgent croaking sound from the frogs. It was as if the whole of the natural world was trying to warn them.

But Jake didn't seem to hear.

CHAPTER FOUR

Next morning, Jake was nowhere to be seen.

"Maybe he's overslept," said Alice.

"Let's go and check." Ben was tense.

As they were climbing the stairs to Jake's bedroom, Alice and Ben heard a strange creaking sound, getting louder and louder. It seemed to be coming from the top of the old house.

Soon the creaking was so loud that their ears hurt.

"What is it?" whispered Ben.

"I don't know," replied Alice fearfully.

Then the creaking suddenly stopped.

"Where was it coming from?" said Alice in a low voice.

"It must have been in the attic. Come on, let's try this door."

They opened it slowly and saw a flight of narrow steps, thick with dust and overhung with cobwebs. Spiders scuttled and then were suddenly still, as if watching them.

"I wish we'd brought a torch," hissed Ben as he pushed open another door at the top of the stairs. All they could see was darkness.

"There might be a light switch." Alice fumbled about on the wall, gasping as she touched a spider's web.

Suddenly she found the switch and a dim light glowed on what seemed to be centuries of junk.

Then the creaking began again.

"I think it's coming from round the back of that wardrobe," whispered Ben at last. "Let's pull it out."

They both hesitated. What, or who, would they find?

Trembling, their mouths so dry they could hardly speak, Ben and Alice stumbled towards the wardrobe. As they dragged it aside, the creaking became louder.

"It's a rocking horse," gasped Alice. "And it's moving on its own."

The paint was chipped, an eye was missing, but still glued to its dusty wooden neck was a long black mane.

Alice ran her hand over the coarse hair. The mane felt real.

"What's the matter?" whispered Ben, watching the rocking horse slow to a halt.

"This is it," she hissed.

"*What*?"

"We've found Black Bess's mane."

Gently, Alice pulled at the shiny black hair which easily slid off the wooden neck.

As they stood there, bewildered, their hearts thumping, Ben and Alice heard a whinny from the stable yard below.

Dashing down the stairs, with Alice clasping the mane, they ran out into the early morning sunshine.

Alan Jones was holding Diamond's bridle. The reins were broken and the horse was rearing up.

Alice suddenly felt freezing cold.

"There's no sign of Jake. Diamond came in on his own." Alan sounded very anxious. "Surely he hasn't tried to jump the Raglan Gap—"

Ben and Alice stared at him in horror, realizing that was just what Jake must have done.

Dragging off Diamond's bridle, Alan quickly shut him in his loose box and ran towards the office. "I'm going to phone the mountain rescue team. You stay here."

But when he had gone, Ben and Alice knew exactly what they had to do.

CHAPTER FIVE

Neither Alice nor Ben had ever ridden so fast in their lives. As Thunder and Lightning raced down the dusty trail, it suddenly seemed as if their hooves barely touched the ground.

When they reached the Raglan Gap the mist was as dense as ever.

Alice and Ben tied Thunder and Lightning to a couple of stunted oaks and then got down on their stomachs, lying on the edge, trying to see if Jake had survived.

But all they could see was mist.

Then, suddenly, they heard the sound of
hooves.

"Bess," yelled Alice. "We've got your
mane!"

There was a snorting sound and then the
pawing of hooves. But they still couldn't see
the ghost horse.

"It's true," shouted Ben. "Come and take a look." But where was Jake, he wondered. Was he already dead? The roaring of water filled his ears.

Then, rising out of the mist, a black shape leapt the gap. For a second Bess seemed to float silently above them before landing safely on the springy turf.

Alice threw the mane at her and watched it swirl in the air until it settled snugly around Bess's neck.

The ghost horse whinnied in delight. As she wheeled round to gallop back towards the gap, the mist began to lift.

By the time she leapt, sunbeams were
filling the chasm, picking out Jake as he lay
on a ledge below, one leg awkwardly splayed
out. He saw them and waved weakly.

"Thanks, Bess," said Alice to herself.
"Thanks for helping us to find Jake alive."

Bess's shadowy shape was on the other side of the Raglan Gap now, cantering away into the distance. Then she disappeared and so did the sound of her hooves. One moment she was there, the next moment she was gone and the bleak, rocky landscape was empty.

"Jake's OK," shouted Ben, as Alan Jones came galloping up.

"What a miracle!" he gasped. "The mist always fills the gap and hardly ever clears. We'd never have seen him otherwise. Now the helicopter can lower someone down."

Ben and Alice sat by Jake's bedside. Fortunately, he only had a broken leg and had been taken to the same hospital as his father.

Just as they'd finished telling Jake all about finding the mane and returning it to Bess, Aunt Megan came running into the ward. When she reached them, she began to weep.

Then she gently took Jake's hand and whispered, "Your dad's just come out of his coma. He's going to be all right."

Thanks again, Bess, thought Alice.

For a moment Alice was sure she could hear galloping hooves outside the hospital window. Then they quietly died away.

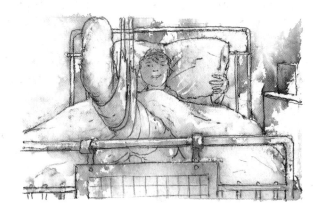

DARE TO BE SCARED!

Are you brave enough to try more titles in the Tremors series? They're guaranteed to chill your spine...

The Ghosts of Golfhawk School by Tessa Potter
Martin and Dan love frightening the younger children at school with scary ghost stories. But then Kirsty arrives. She claims that she can actually see ghosts – and she sees them in so many places that everyone becomes petrified. But she must be lying. After all, ghosts don't exist – do they?

Play... if you dare by Ruth Symes
Josie can hardly believe her luck when she finds the computer game at a car boot sale. "Play... if you dare," the game challenges. So she does. Further and further she plays, each level of the game scarier than the last. Then she reaches the last level. "Play... if you dare," repeats the game. But if she does, she could be trapped for ever...

The Claygate Hound by Jan Dean
On the school camp to Claygate, Billy is determined to scare everyone with his terrifying stories of the Claygate Hound, a vicious ghost dog said to lurk nearby. Ryan and Zeb ignore his warnings and explore the woods, where they find an old ruin covered in ivy. They hear a ghostly howl – and run. Has Billy been speaking the truth, or is there a more terrifying reason for what they have heard?

All these books and many more can be purchased from your local bookseller. For more information about Tremors, write to: The Sales Department, Macdonald Young Books, 61 Western Road, Hove, East Sussex BN3 1JD.